For Mabel
—N. L. & D. E.

For Rachel & Mia
—D. K.

SIMON & SCHUSTER BOOKS FOR YOUNG READERS • An imprint of Simon & Schuster Children's Publishing Division
1230 Avenue of the Americas, New York, New York 10020 • Text copyright © 2015 by Nathan Lane and Devlin Elliott
Illustrations copyright © 2015 by Dan Krall • All rights reserved, including the right of reproduction in whole or in part in any form.
SIMON & SCHUSTER BOOKS FOR YOUNG READERS is a trademark of Simon & Schuster, Inc.
For information about special discounts for bulk purchases, please contact Simon & Schuster Special Sales
at 1-866-506-1949 or business@simonandschuster.com.
The Simon & Schuster Speakers Bureau can bring authors to your live event. For more information or to book an event,
contact the Simon & Schuster Speakers Bureau at 1-866-248-3049 or visit our website at www.simonspeakers.com.
Book design by Lizzy Bromley • The text for this book is set in ITC Berkeley Oldstyle. • The illustrations for this book are rendered in Photoshop.
Manufactured in China • 0415 SCP
2 4 6 8 10 9 7 5 3 1
Library of Congress Cataloging-in-Publication Data • Lane, Nathan, 1956– author.
Naughty Mabel / by Nathan Lane and Devlin Elliott ; illustrations by Dan Krall. — First edition. • pages cm
Summary: "Mabel, the fanciest and sassiest dog the Hamptons has ever seen, causes all sorts of chaos
for her parents with her naughty hijinks"— Provided by publisher.
ISBN 978-1-4814-3022-7 (hardcover) — ISBN 978-1-4814-3023-4 (ebook)
[1. Cats—Fiction. 2. Behavior—Fiction. 3. Hamptons (N.Y.)—Fiction. 4. Humorous stories.] I. Elliott, Devlin, author. II. Krall, Dan, illustrator. III. Title.
PZ7.1.L33Nau 2015 • [E]—dc23 • 2014038140

first
edition

Naughty Mabel

Nathan Lane & Devlin Elliott
Illustrated by Dan Krall

Simon & Schuster Books for Young Readers
New York   London   Toronto   Sydney   New Delhi

Hello, darlings. Allow me to introduce myself. I'm Mabel.
Mabel of the Hamptons. And this is my humble abode.

I know a lady isn't supposed to reveal her age, and we're only on the third page, but I feel like I know you already—

I'm five! Oh, I know I don't look it. Besides, five is the new three!

Anyway, as you can see, life is good, real good. Like a sundae with bacon on top. Or caviar. Ohhh, or peanut butter. But I digress, back to me.

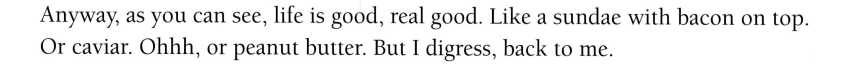

My parents are very sweet, for humans, and take very good care of me.
They have many little pet names for me—Sweetie, Precious, Snookieookums—
but mostly they call me . . .

NAUGHTY!

At first I didn't even know what the word meant.
Honestly. Would I lie to you?

But when I looked it up,
I was flabbergasted.

I am not naughty.

I am VERY naughty.

My parents say I'm a "Frenchie,"

which I find odd as I don't speak French.

I have zero interest in snails . . .

and I look absurd in a beret.

But I do love bread and cheese!

And FRIES!!!

Wait, maybe I am French.

I also like to give kisses to everyone!

And lick everything!

Even myself. . . .

Do you mind, darlings?
This is private.

Now, don't get me wrong, I wouldn't want you
to think I'm—how do you say?—pampered.
I have my jobs to do.

I just like to keep things interesting.

Most of my week is taken up
with napping

and chewing my foot
(don't knock it till you've tried it).

But I love weekends best because that's when we have quality family fun time. And if there's anything that spells quality family fun time, it's MINIATURE GOLF!!

Am I right, people?

Of course, I play by my own rules. I'm a maverick, what can I say?

But this particular weekend I smelled something fishy, and not just because they had sushi for lunch. No, on Saturday, instead of quality family fun time, it was suddenly . . .

BATH TIME!!

Maybe it's the French in me, but I do not like to bathe. Not one bit.

Seriously, people, what's the obsession with soap
and water? Once every three weeks is perfectly fine.

I discussed this new wrinkle in my
routine with my feline friends next door,
Smarty-Cat and Scaredy-Cat.

We all decided that there could only
be one reason for my special bath. . . .

My parents were throwing a party!

Smarty-Cat and Scaredy-Cat were jealous because the humans in *my* life throw fabulous parties, while their human is a nice old lady who falls asleep watching late-night infomercials.

They said I'm lucky as well as naughty. A frightening combination.

UN-lucky is more like it, because that night I was sent to bed early!
Alone, bathed, party-less. . . . This injustice called for a response.

Because I live to party!!!

My game plan was to try to blend in, hoping they wouldn't notice.

They noticed.

So did everyone else. You've never seen so many camera phones flashing. Very red carpet.

I was told parties aren't for naughty little girls. But what good is a party *without* naughty little girls?

I'm a free spirit, and I could not let my parents hold me back.
Drastic times call for drastic measures.

I'm really quite fast, so it was almost impossible for them to catch me.

ALMOST.

Do you know the name
of a good lawyer?

Oh, if my parents only spoke my language,

I would have explained to them that sometimes naughty little girls just aren't ready for bed yet,

and that by the looks of things, this naughty little girl had actually livened up the evening

and turned a so-so party into a rousing success.

YOU'RE WELCOME!

But instead my stomach started growling, and rumbling, and . . .

Darlings, in my defense, I'd eaten far too many pigs in way too many blankets. Unfortunately, the pigs had the last word.

ffffffffffffffffffffffrt...

Well, I sure know how to clear a room.
I guess that was the end of the party.

I thought I was in real
trouble this time.

But that's when my parents told me that even though I had been very unladylike, they loved me anyway, no matter what. That blew my mind. Humans. Go figure.

You know what?
I think they were
glad I crashed
the party.

They get lonely without me.

After all, we are one big, happy family.

So go ahead, call me Naughty Mabel.
My parents do, but that doesn't mean
they love me any less. And I couldn't
love them any more.